THE NIGHT
AT THE MUSEUM

MILAN TRENC

BARRON'S

All inquiries should be addressed to:
Barron's Educational Series, Inc.
250 Wireless Boulevard
Hauppauge, NY 11788
www.barronseduc.com

ISBN-13: 978-0-7641-3631-3
ISBN-10: 0-7641-3631-3

Library of Congress Control Number: 2006924305

Printed in China
9 8 7 6 5 4 3 2 1

Larry was very happy. He had a new job as a night guard at the Museum of Natural History! And he had a wonderful, new uniform with shiny brass buttons. When Larry put it on, he looked like a general, or a policeman, or a pilot!

"Don't worry about the rest of the museum—there are others to take care of it. Just keep an eye on the dinosaurs, and everything will be okay. I'll check on you in the morning."

Larry settled into his chair and stretched his legs. "This is great," he thought. "I'll just close my eyes and relax. There can't be any harm in that." But a moment later, he was fast asleep.

When Larry woke up, he couldn't believe his eyes. The dinosaur skeletons had disappeared! All that was left was a single bone!

He grabbed it and rushed into the corridor. Another guard was there. "Help! Help! We've been robbed! The dinosaurs are missing!" Larry shouted.

"Calm down, there's no need to get excited," the guard comforted him. "They're probably around somewhere. Sometimes they wander off if you're not careful."

"Dinosaur skeletons wandered off?!!" Larry exclaimed. There was definitely something wrong.

In the basement a small train had brought in tons of food for the animals. It carried everything from hay for the elephants and bananas for the monkeys . . .

. . . to meat for the lions and plankton for the whales. While he was looking around, Larry found another huge bone. But the dinosaurs themselves were nowhere to be seen.

"Oh say—while you're here, could you give us a hand unloading?" asked a guard.

After unloading the food, Larry helped the guards feed the animals. When they had finished, one of them said,

"Why don't you look in the park?

. . . And as long as you're going that way, why don't you take the animals from the New York State exhibit with you? They would really enjoy a little walk."

In the park Larry realized he could have been worse off. Other guards had to take the giant octopus and the blue whale for a swim in the lake!

But Larry did find another big bone. The guards in the park suggested . . .

... that he try the mine below the Hall of Gems and Minerals. And, of course, Larry couldn't refuse to bring a snack to the guards working there.

"Oh, the dinosaurs? They were here just a moment ago!" said the guard. "Maybe they went to the planetarium."

In the planetarium the coyotes were practicing
howling at the moon. And of course there was . . .

. . . a little job for Larry. One of the guards asked him to touch up the stars on the ceiling with fluorescent paint.

When he finished, it was almost dawn. Larry was desperate.
He didn't know where to look next. Then he noticed that something
was going on in the museum office.

The statues of John Audubon, the famous bird painter, and the explorers, Lewis and Clark, had stepped down from their usual places above the big front doors. They were enjoying a cup of tea and a game of cards.

"Looking for dinosaurs, little fella?" asked William Clark. "They're in the dinosaur room! In fact, they have been there all night playing hide-and-seek."

It was true! The dinosaurs were really there and not a bone was missing!

"It seems the guards have played the old 'bone trick' on you," said Clark.

"They just scatter some big bones all over the museum.
Then as you collect them, they get you to do their work.
But don't be upset. They do it to every newcomer."
Larry wasn't angry. He just said,

"Well, they won't play that trick on me again—that's for sure!"
Then he looked at his pocket watch.
"Hey, we're opening soon!" He shouted to the dinosaurs.
"Olly-olly-ox-in-free, hurry back to your places!"

Rrrrring! The bell is sounding, the big doors are opening and visitors are pouring in. Everything in the museum is ready: dinosaurs, insects, stars, . . .

. . . minerals, whales, elephants—all fresh and rested. But the night guards are exhausted. They are ready to go to bed!

"You did well tonight," said the chief guard. "Not that you had a tough job napping among the dinosaurs. It's the others that really work hard! So I'd like to ask you for a favor. One of the guards just called in sick. Would you mind taking the day shift as well?"

"I'd be glad to help, sir," Larry said
. . . and collapsed into a chair.

So if you see a guard asleep when you visit the museum, don't wake him up.

He might be recovering from a very difficult night.

6·99
1/07